TABU AND THE
DANCING ELEPHANTS

ELEPHANTS

RETOLD BY *Rene Deetlefs*
ILLUSTRATED BY *Lyn Gilbert*

Dutton Children's Books ◆ New York

CIP Data is available.

Published in the United States 1995
by Dutton Children's Books,
a division of Penguin USA
375 Hudson Street, New York, New York 10014
Published by arrangement with The Inkman,
Cape Town, South Africa.
Designed by Adrian Leichter
Printed in Hong Kong
First Edition
10 9 8 7 6 5 4 3 2 1
ISBN 0-525-45226-5

For my beloved children and grandchildren,
and all who believe in the power of love and the magic of music.
For the African goddess Marimba,
protector of wild animals and maker of marimbas.
R.D.

To Niki Daly,
for his warm friendship and inspired insights,
but most of all for his sense of fun.
L.G.

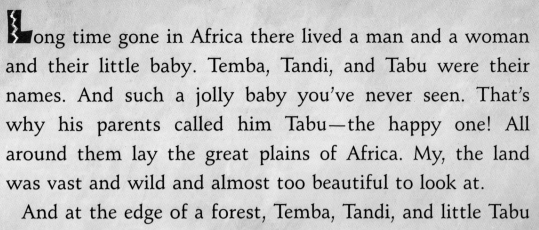

Long time gone in Africa there lived a man and a woman and their little baby. Temba, Tandi, and Tabu were their names. And such a jolly baby you've never seen. That's why his parents called him Tabu—the happy one! All around them lay the great plains of Africa. My, the land was vast and wild and almost too beautiful to look at.

And at the edge of a forest, Temba, Tandi, and little Tabu lived in a mud-and-sticks hut.

It had a fresh dung floor and a neat thatch roof—all made with Mama Tandi's two hardworking hands. And a beautiful hut it was, too! Cool in summer, warm in winter. And didn't Papa Temba just love that!

Every morning as the sun chased away the dark, Tandi took her hoe and went to tend their fields. How that woman worked under the hot, hot sun! She dug and planted, she weeded and hoed, stopping only to wipe the sweat from her brow.

All the while, Temba stayed at home to watch over tiny
Tabu. But that poor man, was he a dreamer! He'd fall
asleep while the pit-pat of Mama Tandi's footsteps still
sounded in his ears. And what a song he made of it as he
snored—*"Grroh…grroh…grroh!"*

But Tabu he did not mind at all. How he admired his papa! Tell me now, who hunted antelope for Tabu to eat? Who carved tiny toy animals for Tabu to play with? Papa Temba, of course! I tell you, Papa Temba was his hero—for sure. So while Papa Temba slept, Tabu played happily with his toy animals until he grew tired and sleepy.

Nearby on the riverbank lived a herd of elephants. Goodness! What a life they had, eating fruit and juicy leaves and bathing in the cool, cool water of the deep, deep river.

Listen, you must believe what I say is true. Every day, from the safety of the forest, an old mama elephant used to watch as Tandi waved good-bye to her family. She saw how Temba would yawn and disappear into the hut, leaving tiny Tabu to play alone in the warm sand. Poor baby! To the mama elephant, he looked just like a lost calf!

Then, one day, the old mama elephant came out of hiding. Well, you should have seen Tabu's face!

An elephant! His favorite animal! The elephant stood be-
fore him, her twinkling eyes looking straight into Tabu's.
Tabu just loved that! For eyes, you know, talk a language
of their own.

Then, gently, the elephant lifted Tabu high with her strong trunk and placed him firmly on her back. Was Tabu afraid? Not at all! Twenty birds sang in his heart as the elephant carried him off and away toward the river!

Mama Tandi returned home in the afternoon. She was tired, but longing to hold her baby. I tell you, just one smile from Tabu could make that woman sing. But what was this? Elephant footprints!

"Tabu!" she cried. "Child of my heart, where are you?" A guinea fowl stuttered, *"K-k-k-kek!"*—which was no answer at all. Mama Tandi peered inside the hut. But only Temba was there, fast asleep. *"Grroh…grroh…grroh!"*

Suddenly, she was scared... *very scared!* She shook Temba and cried, "An elephant has taken our baby!"

Temba shot up. "*Yoooo!* I'll kill those elephants!" he thundered. Grabbing his mighty spear, he dashed off toward the river. Guinea fowl darted this way and that way—out of the man's way.

But the elephants—those clever creatures—caught the sounds of his pounding feet, and his yelling, in their great ears. So, quietly, without breaking the tiniest twig, they hid. You never saw anything like it! Every one of those crafty elephants turned into a rock.

On top of the great mama elephant slept Tabu.

Papa Temba thrashed about by the river like a wounded buffalo. Believe me, you've never heard such a commotion! Clutching his spear, he searched everywhere.

He bumped into rocks.

He skidded on the fallen fruits.

He stumbled over tree trunks—*and other trunks!*

He toppled over stones and nearly tumbled into the river.

That poor man, he was blind with rage! No wonder he could not spot the elephants. No wonder he could not find Tabu. It was dark when Papa Temba, tired and sad, returned to the hut. Mama Tandi was making supper and sobbing, *"Hoooo…hoooo…hoooo!"*

He put his scratched arms around her. "Tomorrow," he promised, "tomorrow I'll find Tabu.…"

And so, with sad hearts, they lay down for the night. But Mama Tandi—she could not close her eyes. Quietly, she got up and took Tabu's little buckskin blanket. By the light of the moon, she hurried down to the river, singing all the while a song for her lost Tabu.

One by one, the elephants—those gentle giants—came out of hiding and stood listening to her song. So sorrowful. So beautiful. They saw the little buckskin blanket, they saw the sadness in her eyes. Snuffling the trail of the baby blanket, the elephants followed Tandi.

Then she stopped and turned around to face them. "Give me back my child, my only one, my Tabu!" she pleaded. Gracefully, the elephants swayed their heads from side to side. Their great trunks moved to a gentle rhythm. They seemed to say, "First fetch your marimba. This is a night for dancing!"

Mama Tandi was overjoyed, her heart was filled with hope! She ran home. How she ran! In no time, she was back with the marimba in her hands. Then Mama Tandi's music filled the night like sparkling water pouring into a dark empty pot.

The elephants trumpeted! They waved their trunks, and all of a sudden...

...on three legs, on two legs, on one leg—every elephant was dancing! You never saw anything like it!

They twisted and twirled, they tumbled and rolled all through the night—until Tandi could play no more.

The first light of day colored the elephants pink, orange, and purple. Then slowly, they stepped aside and formed a passageway. Gracefully, the old mother elephant came forward. On her back sat Tabu! Mama Tandi, was she glad? Why, she wept with joy!

"Mama, Mama!" shouted Tabu happily as he scrambled into the arms of his mama.

The elephants trumpeted and seemed to say, "We'll never forget how we danced tonight!" Then Mama Tandi, with tiny Tabu tied safely to her back, danced all the way home where Papa Temba was just waking up.

Oh, happiness! Papa Temba was as glad as glad can be to see his tiny Tabu! They all laughed and spoke at the same time.

"Dancing elephants? *Yoooo*, never!" gasped Papa Temba. That poor man could not believe a word of it. But you'd better believe it...

...for it is as true as a rabbit in the moon rising over Africa.